Stealing Cherries

also by Marina Rubin

Ode to Hotels

Once

Logic

Stealing Cherries

Marina Rubin

Manic D Press
San Francisco

Published by Manic D Press. For information, contact Manic D Press,
PO Box 410804, San Francisco CA 94141 www.manicdpress.com

Cover photo by Philip Volkers Printed in the USA

Library of Congress Cataloging-in-Publication Data

Rubin, Marina.
[Short stories. Selections]
Stealing cherries / Marina Rubin.
pages cm
ISBN 978-1-933149-80-6 (pbk.) -- ISBN 978-1-933149-81-3 (ebook)
I. Title.
PS3618.U295A6 2013
813'.6--dc23

2013032369

For my brother
Boris

Contents

I

Welcome to America

we arrived at the john f kennedy airport in the middle of april, wearing our heaviest sweaters, astrakhan coats, centuries-old gold refurbished from coins and teeth into earrings and chains. a family of five with no english and two suitcases per person, careers, houses, and tombstones neatly packed between the linings. for hours we stood against the wall with refugees from china, guatemala, and turkey, nibbling on plastic food smuggled in from pan american, waiting for the white cards that one day would become green cards and eventually blue passports. we were driven to our hotel in downtown brooklyn. with tears we watched the country of our dreams in all its magnificence of verrazano, twin towers, and woolworth. the seedy lobby of our court street motel greeted us with its pre-giuliani decadence and the cast of characters from *scarface* and *taxi driver*. we waited for the elevator, our lives assembled in a pyramid. when the doors finally popped open, a homeless black man covered in blood collapsed onto our suitcases in a magnificent drug overdose.

Welcome to America: Day Two

today we were visited by representatives from the salvation army. as if we were survivors of some natural disaster, they brought us food, blankets, sweat suits, t-shirts from the gap, tylenol, excedrin, cough syrup, thrift-store dostoevsky and tolstoy in english. we felt a tinge of shame for our fur coats hanging in the closet, for our rubies, diamonds, and boxes of contraband medication, even for *the idiot* and *war and peace* we had read in its original in high school. in broken english mixed with russian and ukrainian, we tried to tell the nice philanthropic people that we came here not because we were poor but because we were jewish, that we were persecuted, that my brother–a physics wunderkinder–could never study at the russian harvard, that my mother–a top economist–was passed over time and again for that huge promotion. still we took all the books, dishes, and blankets, and put on sweat suits and t-shirts and smiled our grateful all-american smiles because here you just never know how things might turn out.

Welcome to America: The Weekend

we were invited to celebrate passover with a community of hasidic jews in crown heights. we could have been murderers, robbers, imposters. nevertheless, these god's chosen people, forever faithful to their black wool, opened their doors to us without any misgivings. self-effacing families with a gazillion children and barely any furniture fought against rich jewelers and judaica storeowners for the mitzvah of providing our room and board. every day for breakfast, lunch, and dinner we were taken to a different household, presented with mezuzahs, yarmulkes, talmuds of various sizes and bindings. in every doorway women were giving me skirts, gingham skirts to go to yeshiva, ruffled skirts for purim carnivals, skirts for bat mitzvah, skirts for shabbat. they called us *baal teshuva,* the ones who had returned. we sat at their tables, watched them pray, sing, soak apples in honey, toast to meeting next year in jerusalem; without any misgivings, we were finally free to be jewish and yet, even among our own people, we didn't belong.

Welcome to America: The Bag

Emma Schwartz, my mother's lifelong friend, helped us find our first apartment. she knew all the shortcuts of immigrant life, how to sign up for welfare, which store had chicken legs on sale, where to buy yesterday's bread, half price. one night she burst into a grim soliloquy, oy vey America, it is far from the *La Dolce Vita* we expected, a student stabbed for a pair of sneakers, an old woman mugged in broad daylight, earrings torn off with the flesh, bag snatched together with a finger. my mother, terrified, remembered the expensive leather bag she bought in Rome next to the Trevi Fountain, she loved it, but if it was going to cost her her dear life... promptly, she brought the cursed bag into the kitchen, tags still attached, and said, Emmachka, you have been such a wonderful friend, please accept this humble present. next evening, as we sat on the porch watching the mexican vendors roll up their flowers, we saw Emma Schwartz strutting down the street, swinging my mother's bag with the carelessness of an italian schoolgirl.

Welcome to America: Purple Rain

was the first film we had seen in this country. on a television set rescued from the dumpster, we took turns holding up the antenna as we watched Prince, not sure if he was white or black, a man or a woman, Michael Jackson or someone else. he sang ballads and rode a motorcycle without having a job while my brother needed cash for a pineapple so he pasted flyers on poles until one day he carried it in like a kettlebell, opened it, devoured it, then cried like a little boy because it tasted nothing like it did in his dreams. the girls in the movie wore garter belts on stage, their hair wall-like in the front cascaded in a waterfall, we wondered if this was the american fashion we were brave enough to follow. we had no idea why Prince's father shot himself but my father already knew that he would never be a doctor again, a stock boy at the Sunrise 99¢ store he took home Tide that was discarded as trash, accused of stealing he was sacked in the morning. that first desperately hot summer we let the purple rain wash all over us as we strolled the air-conditioned Waldbaums every night in our house slippers, counting the years it would take to try all the variations of cheese.

Otlichnitsa

i grew up among children of military. their fathers, lieutenants and colonels, picked them up from school in green overcoats and government cars. every few years they were stationed at a different army base, in Bulgaria, Hungary, or East Germany. my friends always returned with erasers that smelled of strawberries and tangerines, Adidas suits and Nike sneakers, Bazooka Joes with comic strips, a phenomenon that never reached the counters of Soviet department stores. in the fourth grade we were asked to share with the class what we wanted to be when we grow up. i stood in front of the blackboard, otlichnitsa, overhearing excited screams: astronaut, scientist, brain surgeon. how could i tell them, the children of military, that what i really wanted to be was the wife of some general, not because i cared for men in uniforms, but because of the things, the Adidas, the Nikes, the pencils with little erasers on top, the Yugoslavian bubblegum i could chew night and day, blowing white bubbles until they popped all over my face.

otlichnitsa: student with excellent grades and exceptional public service

Guests

i was eleven and a half the summer we rented a cottage on the shore of the Black Sea. mom could not get away from work so dad became a regular chef boyardee making us garden salads in sour cream. my brother played tennis, dad read newspapers on the beach about Chernobyl, perestroika, a gang of Crimean boys occupied our backyard fixing motorcycles, scooters. one day coming out of the water, i saw blood dripping down my thigh. horrified, i hid in the bathroom recalling stories i heard at the girls pioneer camp about blood coming in every month, like a horde of uninvited but punctual guests. for days i tried to stop the flow with rags secretly washing my underpants in the sink. on the fourth night i could not fight any longer. i whispered into the darkness, dad i am bleeding from down there. a moment of silence then *horosho*, just one word, good. the following morning when i woke up, boxes of maxi pads, tampons, sanitary napkins, cotton balls, and even q-tips sat on my nightstand like some kind of a magical gourmet gift basket.

Zelёnka

i was just as blond and blue-eyed as the other Ukrainian girls who wore little brass Jesuses on their necks and traveled to grandmothers in villages and fed roosters in wooden coops. one day a doctor came to our house, Dr. Krik, his last name meant *scream* in translation. my older brother, a boy of fifteen, recently released from the hospital, was in the living room, sprawled out on the couch wearing loose boxer shorts, sighing and moaning. if i peeked at just the right angle i could see layers of skin, hair and bone, covered in zelënka. the doctor assured everything was healing properly. standing in the sunlight like Moses he said congratulations, young man, you are now a real Jew. with my feet barely reaching the floor, i thought so that's what it means to be a real Jew – zelënka in your underpants, and if my brother was a Jew there was at least a 50% chance that my parents were Jews, and therefore i was 25% Jew. i screamed at my parents, how could you, why didn't you tell me, why were you hiding this from me? they said oh, we knew you'd find out soon enough.

zelënka: antiseptic dye used to prevent infection, in brilliant green color

When the Parents Were Away in Florence

i was thirteen and envious of restless legs pedaling through the italian countryside, i could never ride a bike, something inside me insisted on having both feet on the ground. that spring we lived in the refugee camp on the outskirts of Rome, my grandmother made sweetbread from scratch, my parents dreamed of seeing the David. the night they went away i sat on the porch with our neighbor Arkady who was in his fifties and married to a woman in her twenties and they had three little kids together and he wasn't rich and she married him for love. he put me on the bike and pushed me very carefully and for once i didn't fall, didn't scrape my knees or bruise my arms. i rode my bike past vineyards and groves of olive and almond, it was natural like walking, running, breathing. when my parents returned from Florence, they kept talking about Galileo and Shakespeare who were born the same year that Michelangelo died, and i tried to ride a bike but my feet were tied to the ground with something invisible, strong and raw.

Proposal

everyone knew we were leaving, quitting jobs, selling furniture, surrendering passports. there was a family wedding, our house became the headquarters for out-of-town relatives and guests. my brother came back from the university with a professor's son, Vladimir. we sneaked out during ceremonies, the boring toasts, the ballroom dances, my brother talked about life in the big city, Vladimir read poetry about longing, infinite and all-consuming passion, his voice resonating in the garden of blooming apples. he proposed, said no big-town girl loved his poetry more than this silly goose. i told mama i am getting married. she said, but you are only twelve. i quoted Pushkin, love conquers all ages, she grinned – he wants to go to America, the only way for him is by marriage, and poetry, it will always be just that... poetry. twenty years later, in a box of old letters and bank statements, we found the wedding photo, sixty of us standing on the steps of our small town city hall, like a six-tier chorus. mama pointed to Vladimir, sweetheart you should have married him. i laughed, but mama i was twelve. so what, she said, love conquers all ages.

Dress for the Dog

i asked Nikita Sobakevich, Ukraine's travel agent extraordinaire, to arrange a chauffeur-driven car to Uman. instead he booked a two-bedroom loft in Vinnitsa. drawing skull and bones over his resume, i reiterated that i need a car with a driver and an air-conditioner. in response he sent me photos of the sunlit living room, a bedroom done in kitsch Versace style. for weeks as we continued arguing, my friends, acquaintances and co-workers gathered parcels for their loved ones overseas, heart medication for ailing great-grandmothers, blue onesies for newborn babies, pushup bras for unmarried glamour girls, money for gravestone caretakers. and then Nikita Sobakevich called, he too needed a package delivered from United States. out of curiosity i asked what was in it – a pair of sweatpants, a bathing suit, and a dress for the dog, he replied. as i packed my suitcase full of dresses, strapless, off the shoulder, asymmetrical, i thought perhaps i should have taken the dress for the dog, god forbid there was a German Shepherd wandering the slums of Vinnitsa, butt-naked.

The House

my grandparents bought this property when they got married in 1945, a second chance, they built, installed, connected, planted until it was a mansion with pear and apple orchards, glorious gazebos, dreamy lilac bushes. i returned to my childhood home to find the blue picket fence replaced by a gate with barbed wire and a sign "we buy metal at top prices." a man in a tiny speedo with a money belt across his bulging belly unbolted many locks, i told him i was born in this house, my mother was born in this house, we left this house twenty years ago. he invited me inside, a wasteland of scrap metal, a junkyard of steel rods and beams, rusty refrigerators and crushed cars. an industrialist wanna-be, with great gusto and delight, he told me all about the bulldozer he hired to bring the old house down, the demolition crew that ripped out all the trees, and the luxury high-rise he was planning with apartments for rent at eight hundred a month. in the shack that was once my kitchen, he offered me beer and bitter pickles, boasting that he already received permission from the city for a modest helicopter landing on the roof of his imaginary building.

Childhood Friend

they warned me about her. the prettiest little girl on our street, she was now a drug addict, a drunk. messy divorce, house full of thugs, mother's throat slit at a party, they barely saved her. i went to our playground, listened to the echo of all-important girlish gossip, the secrets of childhood sweethearts. i called, asked her to come downstairs for a minute, a surprise. she sent her boyfriend to check it out and when he saw that there was no jeep of kidnappers waiting outside, she came, my bosom friend, my partner in crimes of discovering lipstick, skeletal, with blood-shot eyes and yellow fingertips, a lip mustache, smelling of vodka at four in the afternoon. we sat on the bench next to the orange seesaw and the tire swings, twenty years since we had seen each other last, she held my hand, wavering between recognition and forgetfulness. it was her birthday. her mother, a scarf tied around her neck, kept shrieking out that it was time to make the salad, serve the herring. we exchanged our numbers, certain that i will never call and she will lose that piece of paper before she makes it past the monkey bars.

Judaism for Dummies

they studied mathematics in downtown university, my brother Boris and his classmate Michael, a red-haired boy who wore a yarmulke and read *Judaism for Dummies*. they became friends, Michael invited Boris to a Shabbat celebration. on Friday before sundown they took a train to Borough Park, lit candles at the synagogue, recited kiddush over a cup of wine, broke challah with the rabbi who called them Moses and Baruch. after dinner the boys came back to Michael's place only to find his living room illuminated like Carnegie Hall. Michael cried he can't turn off the lights on Shabbat, quoted the Talmud, read excerpts from his *Judaism for Dummies*. my brother tried to fall asleep, tossing, turning, suffocating in the carnival of lights, while Michael lay in the darkness of his bedroom, praying for an answer. in the middle of the night on Shabbat, the time of rest and meditation, Moses and Baruch, like burlaks on the river Volga, were pulling the enormous couch from the living room into a tiny bedroom.

A Yiddishe Momme

since the day of his Bar Mitzvah she had embarked on a crusade to find her son a wife. time was of the essence, she was certain that if a man does not get married by the age of twenty-eight, sperm will clop him in the head, making him a raving idiot. she worried he might become a shlepper in short crinkled trousers, or fall prey to some skinny goyka go-go dancing on the tables, or a divorced haika with two children and a GED. a garrulous, fierce woman, she consulted every marriage broker in Brooklyn, placed ads in local papers, Jdate, Frumster, asked for referrals at the Torah study group, everything, short of cementing posters on trees and light poles, dumping flyers from a hired chopper. then one day she was hit by a car, it was a miracle she survived, broke her collarbone, jaw, and six ribs. a month later she fell and broke both her legs. laid up like a mummy in a white body cast, a yiddishe momme gave up her search and accepted defeat, and just then, standing above her, checking IVs was a new resident doctor, a sheyne maideleh she always pictured for her sweet boy.

Babushka

till the day she died at the age of ninety-four, she wore perfume, silk hose, a brooch of rubies, a triangle scarf. she went down to the park, why don't you find yourself a boyfriend, i pestered her all the time, so many cute available grandpas playing checkers and chess. are you kidding me, she would reply, those old farts! she spent her evenings polishing silver forks, spoons, knives, muttering proudly that once upon a time this was her inheritance and now my dowry. on her deathbed she called me over, pulled me close, with the passion and frenzy of a long-awaited confession she blurted out, i am one hundred years old but don't tell anyone. i left the room and told everyone, but they all said not to worry, that grandma was just senile, losing her mind, imagining things. on the way to the cemetery, i kept staring ahead at the hearse where she traveled alone like a queen, as our family followed in a procession of lincolns; no, grandma wasn't senile at all, she really was a hundred years old, with pogroms, revolutions, wars, houses burned, husbands died, papers vanished. to shave off six, seven years was a charming indiscretion in the story of a woman.

Mother-in-Law

i found a watch on a thin gold bracelet. years later, the identical watch, on a worn leather band. i fastened them together, tied like a hand-tefillin, two watches on parallel lines, two grandmothers with the same watch. one who died at fifty-three, leaving my father alone, Cinderella to his father's several wives. the other lived for almost a century, letting my mother remain a child long into her sixties. my parents both orphans now. in their oversized nightgowns and breeches, drooping chins, mandatory six-month check-ups, sudden interest in politics and soap operas. i imagined myself as an enormous white bird hovering over them with a blanket of wings. they began calling me mother-in-law, i kept meddling in, what to wear, who is unkind, who should apologize. mother screamed get your own husband, father said i was the evil mother-in-law he never had. once we were in a car, father driving mother next to him, their muffled voices, i closed my eyes for a second, forgot my mother-in-law duties, watchfulness, suspicion, and fell asleep like a drooling diaper-clad baby, with the kind of abandon that is only possible of someone whose parents are alive.

Men

they sat at the dinner table with flaming eyes and the courage of a thousand soldiers cleaning their bayonets and going off to war. my cousin leaving behind a wife six months pregnant and a two-year-old son, catching three connecting flights to Johannesburg and one freight locomotive with sheep and industrial plastic. my brother, a Wall Street workaholic faking a hip injury to work from home, locking himself inside the basement, proudly calling it "the sports center," barring women, children, and babysitters. my father abandoning the library, the synagogue, the swimming pool in favor of the couch and a flat screen TV. World Cup 2010, thirty-two teams, sixty-four games, three games per day, ninety-eight hours, five thousand eight hundred fifty minutes, two-hour break to go to the bathroom and get food. i took pity on the three men in the kitchen and offered them my brilliant out-of-the-box idea, instead of suffering through all these games why not watch just one – the finals... i left quietly, a misunderstood Joan of Arc, but on my way out, hovering in the living room i saw my mother and sisters-in-law give me a very secret enthusiastic thumbs-up.

II

Announcement

the blue-eyed college senior came back from Europe ecstatic, full of stories, adventures. her family threw a lavish welcome home dinner, her papa, a doctor, proposed a toast to his little girl, independent and fearless who traveled the world all by herself. and she, in the spirit of celebration or youthful naiveté, asked to raise a glass to her virginity left on the sidewalks of Amsterdam. her papa's champagne slipped to the floor, he grew as white as a doctor's gown, her older brother gave a loud abrupt chuckle hiding his face in his hands, her mama still wearing the large stove mittens holding the chicken pan asked flabbergasted, so now you are getting married? no, of course not the student replied, even more flabbergasted. her papa reclined backwards about to faint, her brother unable to contain himself exploded with laughter, and her 87-year-old grandmama who sat quietly at the end of the table all this time began to panic – i don't understand, what did she say, what did she say? can someone explain all of this to me, no one tells me anything in this family.

Mediterranean Tattoo

eight cities in twelve days, my roommate Lindsey Underwood from Skokie, Illinois dreamed of getting a tattoo. i could never understand her fascination, prisoners had tattoos, truck drivers, bikers, hip hop artists; you get old, your skin sags, you can't get buried in a Jewish cemetery. yet Lindsey was determined, passionate in her quest for the perfect label, the kind that would rest across her body like flamenco, corrida, Gaudi's stones, the clocks of Dali and Chagall's flying lovers. decked in pajamas, in our twin beds, her final words before slumber were always a sweet lullaby i am going to get a tattoo, tattoo, tattoo... last day of our journey, she begged me to come to the tattoo parlor she found in the center of Nice where artists were clean and crisp, like doctors. poor Lindsey Underwood from Skokie, Illinois stood in line, and cried, and cried, and cried because she had a horrid phobia of needles, and i was the one who got the tattoo, because somebody had to, and the Jewish cemetery could wait.

The Green Fairy

i picked a people-watching seat at a café next to Notre Dame, ordered a cappuccino and a spicy chicken tandoori salad, went to the bathroom. when i returned my cappuccino was already waiting, together with a tall glass tube of some kind of a luminous substance. how fabulous, i thought, a little something to cheer me up, a midnight aperitif, or better yet *la fée verte,* the green fairy. in a land of Degas and Toulouse-Lautrec, could they be serving absinthe as if it was pasteurized milk? i poured the mystery tonic into my cappuccino, gulped it down, amazed at its sophisticated slightly bitter taste. everything looked pretty. the homely French couple slurping on fat oysters and even fatter mussels at the next table invited me to join them in a *ménage a trois.* i wondered if i was already hallucinating. i motioned for my waiter to come over, pointing at the glass tube i asked in my most intimate conspiratorial whisper what is in it. oh, that's the dressing, mademoiselle, your salad will be here in just a moment.

Passport

we ate lunch on the grass in Borodino, laughing, photographing our mates in their dramatic reenactment of the famous battle scene. before hitting the road we used the bathroom – a barn with a hole in the ground. we caroled U2 songs all the way to Smolensk when one of our tour mates announced his passport was missing, last seen this morning in his back pocket. our bus stopped. in a frenzy we searched all overhead compartments, underneath the seats, in the aisles, the luggage, the garbage. we had to retrace our steps, return to Borodino, rummage behind Napoleon and Kutuzov, but there it was as we feared, in the barn, in the hole, on the pile of shit, open, with a New Zealand insignia facing upward. we broke up in teams, Canadian programmers constructed a fishing rod, Australian carpenters worked in shifts wearing bandanas on their faces, British kindergarten teachers transported the unfortunate document back to the bus, American CPAs hosed it off. at the Russian border with Poland, a fat woman in passport control went through every page of every passport, licking her index finger.

Moscow Misdemeanors

it was hard to blend in, twenty-seven of us marching together, Australian kangaroos on our backpacks. we checked into hotel Izmailovo located next to chechen markets, the plan was simple: unpack, meet up for a quick drink at the hotel bar, then head out for a Moscow night city tour. but one Stolichnaya led to another until we were flying in our rented loafers down slippery lanes of the bowling alley. Nina lost her wallet, notified security, a swat team of bluecoats arrived almost within minutes, handcuffed Jason who wore Nina's wallet around his neck, like Shaka Zulu. we pleaded with the overzealous task force, they demanded to see passports, Olga in reception refused to give them up without our tour guide present. a multilingual cursing match progressed to a barbaric brawl, as chechen merchants dwelling in the lobby cheered, some for the home team, some for the visitors. bloody and bruised, we watched the Moscow night in all its splendor of golden spires and onion domes through the window of a moving prison bus, the charges against us piling up – theft, assault, public drunkenness. someone mentioned twenty-seven years in Siberia.

the beautiful eighteen-year-old Elena celebrated her birthday at the local disco Red October in Vorkuta, a coal mining city on the tip of North Pole. she dropped off her coat and winter galoshes at the coat check, put on delicate cinderellas and danced all night. before closing she was told that the coat check was burglarized and her galoshes along with another guest's fur hat were stolen. the wrinkled little babushka sat in the corner quietly sobbing. Elena waited in the manager's office with Alexander, a twenty-two-year-old mechanical engineering student who loved his fur hat because the entire political bureau of the Union wore them as they waved from the podiums of the Kremlin. the city militia arrived two hours later, questioned all staff, took statements, declared that the crime rate was down by seventeen percent. Elena and Alexander went out into the infamous Russian winter, barefoot and hatless. three months later they were married.

Women

they descend on Berkshires like sparrows, with their *Eat Pray Loves* and *O* magazines, singles, divorcées, widows, all in search of their inner goddess. Achilla the She-God teaches them warrior poses, how to claim space, manifest love, the power of the yoni. she is graceful, invincible, it is only later when she autographs their books, her eyes, large lonely orbits, like those of a sick dog. they wake at dawn like soldiers at reveille, march up a mountain, praising father sky, lay down on ice, praising mother earth. there are healing rituals, daily affirmations, afternoons spent in back-breaking yoga exercises and tearful hip-openers, karate-chopping of wooden blocks, tap of a foot, strike of a hand. at night in the jacuzzi they agree they have it all, fabulous lives, fabulous shoes, money, freedom. bubbles beat against their backs as they chant i am a 21st century goddess. next day they stand deep in a forest, a woman to a tree, nose and navel pressed to a trunk, hugging the tree with a passion of a lover, tenderness of a parent, snow falling.

Ode to Boots

black leather knee-high boots with a four-inch platform, inside zippers, big round toes. my co-workers called them Herman Munster shoes. i bought them years ago in the village the day i met the perfect man, he never called but these boots stayed. my friends dubbed me Bride of Frankenstein. i didn't care. i was no one's bride on Christmas noon staring into the deep pink spiral of rocks known as the Grand Canyon, something pulling me down there without bottled water, knife or signal mirror. in my big black boots i followed the Bright Angel trail spellbound by pebbles, stones, boulders, yellow, orange, red, five million years, life is small within the fissure of infinite life. i met other voyagers on my path, tired, happy, dusty, of all ages, wishing Merry Christmas, testing the limits of their echo in the canyon. i traveled down three miles and came back without a helicopter, or a mule. my monster boots covered in dirt, wrinkled with a broken zipper, quietly, not asking for applause, carried me all the way; not once did they stumble, give way to earth, betray me like delicate beautiful things. they served, these warrior boots. salute.

Massage in Luxor

i spent the day tomb-hopping from Tutankhamen to Cleopatra, Ramses to Nefertari, every bone in my body aching with glories of history. back at the hotel oasis, away from temples and pharaohs, i decided to treat myself to an aroma therapy massage. a masculine arabic man at the spa took me into the backroom that smelled of cinnamon and nutmeg, put on chimes music, softly almost whispering asked me to undress, lie down on the table and cover myself with a towel. in slow soothing strokes he rubbed jasmine, almond, lavender on my spine, neck, preaching that these oils extracted from plants are the soul of the plant, now i will become light and carefree, like the plant. suddenly the lights in the room went out, the entire oasis turned ebony black, the man started screaming, waving his illuminated cell phone in my face, please don't be afraid it's just a black-out. i tried to get up to reassure him i am not afraid, my towel slipping to the floor. he backed into a corner, shaking senselessly, you stay away from me American woman.

The Palace

a certain five-star hotel in the diplomatic area of New Delhi lost my reservation. as a courtesy i was upgraded to the penthouse. that's where Nicolas Sarkozy stays when he is in town, winked the indian madonna at the front desk. like a maharaja's palace, my suite had a stadium-sized bed, a kitchen stocked with wines and rasmalai, a dozen terrycloth robes, a sixty-inch flat screen. in the bathroom of a million gadgets and buttons, lotions and towels, i undressed, turned on the shower but to my surprise there was no water, i tried the other knob, nothing, i pressed the corresponding button, not a drop. like a child in the elevator, i started pushing all the buttons – the night lamps flickered, the curtains opened, the blinds went up, the fax began to buzz, the teapot whistled. in the wee hours of morning, as i lost my fight against technology-at-the-edge-of-science-fiction, i shampooed my hair in the sink, washed my feet in the bidet and went to sleep, wondering if Nicolas Sarkozy had to do the same thing.

Leaving New Delhi

among mascaras and lipsticks, powders and make-up brushes, two airport security officers found my grandmother's eyebrow tweezers. i refused to give them up, said i am a white woman traveling with an American passport, do you think i plan to stab the pilot with a pair of tweezers? they stood with stern faces of Pakistani freedom fighters, pointing to the airport-issued lethal weapons chart. i tried my best girlish giggle – these are the only tweezers that don't hurt; a crowd of barefoot passengers behind me, complaining. just when i thought, forget the stupid tweezers, i saw the boxes of confiscated tubes of toothpaste, nail files and pocket scissors. i remembered my grandmother in the sunlight of her Coney Island bedroom with a magnifying glass, plucking her eyebrows into a thin slightly surprised line. in this graveyard of utensils, three months after her funeral, i cried my first real tears of grief. the tired Sikh security chief put the tweezers back into my bag, motioned to the others to let the crazy lady through.

Gypsy Cab

it had begun to snow over Moscow. a short round woman in her sixties stood at the curb trying to flag down a taxi. she was hoping that some poor engineer with three kids and three jobs in a beat-up Lada would agree to drive her across town for two hundred rubles, all she had left till her next pension. as Volkswagens and Toyotas, their windshield wipers dancing, passed her, she thought about the hip replacement surgery the doctors had advised her on for years. then a shiny black Mercedes stopped, two hundred? she inquired, get in, the driver nodded. a well-dressed twenty-something fellow, he didn't flinch when she gave him the address, silent, they floated through the gloomy snowed-in boulevards, as if in a barge. when they pulled up to her building he reached for his wallet, counted two hundred dollars, shall we go up? here is the money up-front. baffled, folding unfolding her rubles in creased hands she began crossing herself, Dear God, Jesus Christ, Mary and Joseph, then spitting, hitting him on the head with her bag, have you no shame, little sonny, i am old enough to be your mother. he just shrugged, a shy clumsy smile, well, i was thinking more like my grandmother.

*two hundred rubles is approximately seven dollars

III

we flew to Vegas on the spur of the moment grabbed a taxi from the airport checked into hotel Circus Circus and didn't leave the room for four days. cooped up inside we read and practiced the art of Kama Sutra alternating between the Pillow Book and the self-help manual of sexual positions for the very flexible yogis. we raided the mini bar, ordered room service around the clock, refused a change of sheets and towels, the "do not disturb" sign hung on our doorknob like a banner, defying our parents who worried that we might get married or waste our tuition money on the slot machines. we saw the rays of sun only in the cab on the way back to the airport. driving through the strip, Tropicana, the roaring lions of MGM, abandoned ships of Treasure Island, fountains of Bellagio that shot up into the sky to the music of Rachmaninov and Offenbach, we looked at each other and we knew it was over. we would have been better off taking a room at the Harbor Motor Inn, that dump just off the Belt Parkway in Brooklyn, where they charge by the hour and its cardboard walls are covered with the spunk of truck drivers and pimply teenagers.

The Yarmulke

a friend, who moved away to Minnesota years ago, returned, suddenly religious and more handsome than ever. we met up at an art café in Prospect Park; i devoured pork dumplings with feta cheese while he knocked back bottles of Perrier, the only kosher item on the menu. the sanctuary of his yarmulke made me open like a lotus flower, letting him into my secret crannies, the anthology of heartbreaks, the comical-to-tears affairs. i tried to imagine him without the yarmulke, without the cardigan he was wearing like a retired Harvard professor, the dress shirt, the fruit-of-the-loom tee peeking from under layers of clothing. i imagined him wearing nothing at all, or maybe just the yarmulke. like a perfect gentleman, he picked up the tab, drove me home and as we stood outside saying goodnight, the wind blew so hard his yarmulke landed at my feet. he had the puzzled look of a man who needed to consult his rabbi, but i picked it up, hoping that this was just a phase, like bungee-jumping or LSD, and that next year he might be into horses, vegan foods, Woody Allen, and me, God willing.

The Cleaning Lady

like a phantom Mr. Clean she came over once every two weeks, polished the old creaking parquet, swept the dust off the foreign fiction, scrubbed the sink, changed the sheets, placed chocolates on my pillow, and along with an envelope of three twenties, left. a lovely Polish woman with a crucifix, how sorry she was when she broke a vase and offered to pay for it, months later she quit because she was going to college to pursue a degree in Biology. one night in bed, massaging honey & shea butter over my thighs i mentioned to my lover that i was searching for a cleaning lady. we had been together for what seemed like three million years, without once having a serious conversation, we lived on love and stale chicken tabak. a gorgeous man with an incredible body and an insatiable appetite, he inquired how much i was paying and when i told him sixty dollars, he immediately offered to be my cleaning lady. paralyzed by pity and horror, i stared back at my beautiful lover, pressed my lips together and said nothing.

Bordeaux and Other Mysteries

he called after midnight, said he must see me tonight, we had indulged in a mild flirtation over the years but nothing ever materialized. now he stood in my hallway with a bottle of wine, tall, blond with blue almost albino eyes. i smiled coyly, i don't drink, don't even own a corkscrew. he went on to examine my books, figurines, paintings, then curled up on the loveseat asking about my childhood, my cooking skills, if i am a recovering alcoholic. at four o'clock in the morning he gave me a light peck on the cheek, praised my hospitality and left. i stood in the doorway, utterly stunned, what was that, a booty call gone shy, a lonely visit from a lonely friend, a surprise marriage quiz? weeks later i went to a bohemian gala, brought his bottle of wine as a gift. oh, how the chichi hostess in a handkerchief dress came running across the room, screaming at the guest who tried to open my bottle, don't touch that one, that's a five hundred dollar haut-brion.

Citarella

i came to seduce the artist. under the pretense of buying his art. around the corner at Citarella, i handpicked more than a dozen strawberries. six-fifty a piece, they were strawberries on steroids richly covered in dark, milk, white chocolate, glazed with a gold thread, on a bed of gauze tissues they looked like Faberge eggs. i handed him the gift box in the doorway, for the great maestro, his atelier – a closet without windows, beds or chairs, stale smell of farts, cigarettes and paints, miniature refrigerator in the center doubling as coffee table. among unfinished watercolors, framed prints, rolled canvases like carpets, i heard him remark he hated strawberries, hated chocolate even more, that this was the most unfortunate combination. yet he gobbled them one after another, juice spurting down his chin, chunks of chocolate like pieces breaking off an iceberg, falling to the floor, he picked them up, put them back in his mouth, complaining how costly Citarella was, how he only went there as if for a gastronomical fashion show. i bought two prints i did not need, tramped home through Bryant Park tugging at my disappointment like a new garter belt.

Lovely Feast

he picked me up at my office on Wall Street in his black BMW, a dark and handsome tax attorney i met on the internet. he made dinner reservations at a lavish Zagat-rated bistro in Tribeca with garlands of fresh freesia on the tables and a trio of violinists playing *La Vie En Rose*. we ordered filet mignon, quails in raspberry sauce, a bottle of 1985 Sauvignon, he leaned over and said this place is famous for their hazelnut soufflé. we ate duck pate on french crackers, i asked if he had ever been married, he said no. children? it's complicated, he replied. oh, i said. he met a girl, she got pregnant, he proposed, she said no. oh, i repeated. look, he yelled, turning crimson and crushing crackers in his fist, that bitch used me, she used me for my sperm. stockbrokers, waiters, the anniversary banquet next to us growing dead silent. oh, i murmured. on my way home, i dreamt about the cold fried chicken in my fridge i could eat tonight, without a side of sperm.

Paypal

vice president of japanese equities, once upon a time my lover, invited me out to lunch. between his stir-fried noodles and my beef negimaki he boasted about the pile of cash he had amassed in the foreign markets. with a gallant wave of a hand and a fixed-income smile he said, sweetheart why don't you pick up the tab and then send me a PayPal request for my share? paypal paypal with bits of wasabi and ginger fumed in my mouth as i tried to register, through secure servers, reading instructions, verifying passwords, bank accounts, screaming at the technical support. there was no response the next day or the following morning. like a woman possessed, a prize fighter for principle, an urban samurai, i sent the vice president a Reminder PayPal Request, followed by four more requests, an online warning, an angry voicemail, and a threatening letter. three weeks later i received a PayPal credit for twelve dollars and forty-six cents from my lunch buddy, but there was no satisfaction in this little victory.

Glutton

he wrote books and books of poetry about politics and food, how to end apartheid with a lamb shank, devour a crème brulee for the children in Darfur, binge-eat against atrocities of capitalism. we met for coffee at the Plaza Hotel bar where he kept talking about Joseph Brodsky who was spending eternity with the worst anti-semite Ezra Pound. he ordered a beet salad with rosettes of goat cheese and raved about a top chef who committed suicide in France because he lost a star in last year's ratings. i hugged my silent cup of coffee as he continued with a platter of fried calamari, squeezing lemon in every direction he raged about Afghanistan and the Taliban-enforced rule of heterosexuality. he gobbled up an entrée of honey-glazed chicken with potato skins, a mouthful of Che Guevara, Fidel Castro, and Franz Kafka. he was still feasting on profiteroles soaked in white chocolate syrup when the bill arrived, he was about to have a heart attack but collected himself quickly – hey, i am no scrooge when it comes to ladies.

Sexy Poet From Oakland

a sexy poet from Oakland was giving a reading at the Bowery Poetry Club. it was so refreshing to see a handsome man in a dark suit and a blue button-down shirt slightly open, standing in the spotlight tall and magnificent unlike most of the hippie beatniks who staggered on stage in rags rescued from the back closet of a vintage store in Brooklyn. his poetry was not about unrequited boyish crushes, gay erotica, the alcoholic mother, or incomprehensible rantings from the MFA program but an exciting medley of testosterone-filled adventures of the Bond-like character who races fast cars and hangs out in casinos. i bought his book, he signed it *for a beautiful woman who had made a humble poet blush.* we were invited to a house party, he kissed my hand, said he will go only if i will. a jolly gang of twenty, we separated into different taxis. from Lower East side to Harlem, a hundred blocks in New York city traffic was apparently too long because when i arrived in Harlem the sexy man from Oakland was already kissing another woman on the staircase, some skanky-looking minstrel in vintage garments.

Nothingness and Fullness

i wanted to write the perfect poem. let it be a gory epic of empires sinking, of kings slaughtered, children strangled, of heads drooping from the castle gates, madmen saluting and women unpinning their pins to lie down in a box of prunes. no! that verse across the invincible river must be of ordinary things, parakeets and hamsters that never show signs of aging until one day their home is a shoebox in the sky. more artful than silence, it must be a collage of nothingness and fullness, cherries, the red geraniums, the hands and eyes, the plastic bag pirouetting in a leafless garden, the barrel, the black bed, love. that smoldering day in August when he stood waiting for me in the lobby in an oversized winter coat, his hand wrapped in a white bath towel, a suitcase and a painting he stole from his father that said "rejoice human heart, in God" and i told him i was seeing someone and i watched him spray cologne on his feet and lie about visiting friends in New York.

Confessions of Love

in the summer of '89 everyone loved Ruslan. he was a 14-year-old Brad Pitt, a 40-year-old John Wayne, taking off his shirt, climbing through the windows, diving into the apartments of forgotten keys, scouting the roofs for wounded pigeons and mistaken cats. he was cool, the way only a boy raised by his mother who has to become the man of the house, could be. we waited, in our city of Vinnitsa, pronounced in russian almost like Venice, waited for him every night on the bench in the park to hear his heart-tearing seven-string guitar and every morning in our marilyn bikinis we watched his breaststroke as he crossed the river. i would not dare to love him, he was loved by too many, i was there for my friends, the talk of training bras, mascara stolen from mothers and sisters. walking home one night i heard someone whisper my name. it was Ruslan sitting on top of a tree, stealing cherries. he said he loved me for a long time with all his heart in this entire city of Venice, he loved only me and Luda Vishnevska, whose last name meant black cherry.

The Nest

we were 20 and almost not virgins on New Year's Eve of '98. that year we learned to open doors with our legs and sashay into a room until there were no rooms without men eager to pay our tuition or drive us to Angelica. we welcomed the New Year at a nightclub but by 2am we were so bored a friend who plays the accordion invited us to a splendid soiree in Brooklyn. the mansion in Brooklyn had Chippendale chairs, Persian rugs, and dozens, dozens of men of such manliness, we gasped. there were some women as well, but they were either nieces or aunts, sixty or twelve. we sat on the davenport and struck nonchalant poses of seduction, hours passed without anyone taking notice. infuriated, we turned to our accordion friend – what is going on here? girls, don't you get it, we are right in the nest of Russian homosexuality. we just sat there, gasping, 20, almost not virgins.

Punishment

he left his astroboy email account open as he went downstairs to drop off two suitcases of laundry i've been collecting for months. in his sent folder i stumbled on a note he wrote to Vicky Grapeess, a model turned curator with some proposal for an art installation. when he returned i pointed my finger at the evidence and accused him of cheating, using this opportunity to remind him of every miniscule thing he had ever done wrong. i continued screaming even in the intervals he requested to walk to the basement to move my clothes from washer to dryer, and bring them back. staring at the two bulging suitcases i told him he is punished – he must take every piece of clothing, put it on a separate hanger and place it back in the closet. like an obedient child, or a professional shopper, i watched him smooth out every tank top, every dress. i hope you are thinking about your crime, i hissed. no i am not thinking about it, he replied. i am thinking about how you look in all these clothes.

Potpourri

we heard about the beach on the other side of the resort: the sign prohibiting all photographs, the mandate to remove clothing at the gate within thirty seconds or leave immediately. the nudists, we were not like those people, polite and proper we stayed on the prude beach in our bathing suits, discussing politics and the importance of potpourri. by sundown we knew that there would always be just the two of us on this deserted island, as if in the aftermath of a catastrophe, we were the only remaining humans. somewhere out there, hundreds and hundreds of people sporting nothing but sunscreen, sunglasses, sombreros played volleyball, water badminton, ping pong in pairs. legs, arms, balls, breasts, some silicone, some drooping, swinging in a liberated dance of limbs, a return to ancestral truths. we spat on our principles, we embraced those people, we became those people, for the next eight days we wore nakedness like a luxurious Burberry coat. when it was over, stranded at the Montego Bay airport it pinched our eyes to see all those fully dressed people, and every inseam, every cross-stitch, felt like a cut of a blade, fabric like sandpaper.

Hedonism

at the nudist colony in the land of Ya-Man i had dinner with my lover and his wife. she was a fidgeting little thing with limp black hair, eyes a little too close together, starved pointy shoulders. and when he went to the buffet to get the three musketeers – a plate of beef, lamb and shrimp – she whispered that he has affairs. i asked her, why don't you leave? she said i have nowhere to go. when she went to the buffet, he looked at me and said how strange it is us having dinner together, and i said what is so strange about it, was there anything between us? he said, well, yes of course, don't you remember just last night i walked you home from the hot tub in the valley of palms completely naked and you laughed like a little girl how none of your dates had ever done that before and then... oh yes, i shrugged, sorry i must have forgotten. that night i wrote in my journal – i felt incredible pity for her and still passion for him.

Curious Things at the W Hotel

i had a blind date with a doctor, born and raised in Connecticut, Cornell undergrad, Yale medical school. we met for drinks at the W hotel. he looked like a Roman gladiator about to fight lions rather than a tired emergency room doctor coming off his shift. we exchanged pleasantries about the weather, he said i was beautiful, i told him he was. a stunning couple rushing towards the elevators waved to us, his patients i assumed. a handsome gentleman at the bar wearing a cashmere jacket asked for his bill, shook hands with my doctor, promised to see us later, what a friendly guy i thought. a remarkably attractive woman with a Chanel clutch greeted us in a french accent, caressed my cheek, said she can't wait to see me tonight. a freak case of mistaken identity i noted. a little after eight he looked at his watch, slowly almost hypnotically said we must go now, we are expected at an orgy on the eleventh floor, you will love it, beautiful people, old money, new money, Park Avenue crowd, like in *Eyes Wide Shut.*

IV

The House of Culture

Bug disappeared in the crowd, recently she had been in a car accident and the doctors prescribed her a spinal corset with steel braces, she wore it proudly on top of her clothes and told everyone she had been bitten by an alligator. the opening night at the House of Culture gathered the neighborhood's crème de la crème. i ate six sorts of cheeses, spoke to a dentist, his wife, her manicurist. Bug found me on the sidewalk waiting for the bus, she said her friend who looked like Benicio Del Toro would drive me home. she called me the next night surprised that Del Toro look-alike returned to the House of Culture so fast, she was hoping i would keep him, but not to worry, she gave him my number. really, i said, well what does he do for a living? he makes rolls of money, she replied, has a great car, an oceanfront condo, his hours are really flexible and there are great career opportunities in his trade. sounds great but what does he do? just don't be so stuck-up, he is my drug dealer.

Kopal's Towel

my friend Mouse and her lover Kopal, a downtown performance artist barged in on me one night and asked to use my bedroom. i slept on the couch oblivious to their synchronized enthusiastic moaning. after they left i took a shower but could not find my bath towel. i asked Mouse if she had taken it by chance, she said no but maybe Kopal. i followed up with her a week later, she said they broke up, something about his $300 Diesel underwear and she refused to call about my stupid towel because she had her pride. in the fall i ran into Kopal at CBGB, asked him point-blank, Kopal, did you take my towel? he denied it, said it was ludicrous to even suggest it. in the spring i saw him roller-blading in Central Park, i chased after him. Kopal, you bastard, i know you stole my towel, what kind of man fucks in a stranger's house then steals a stranger's towel? by wintertime i wore him down, he confessed, said he can give me a brand new towel he just stole from somebody else, with VIAGRA written across it.

Ship of Fools

i had boarded a Circle Line cruise from Sheepshead Bay to the South Street Seaport in hopes of seeing Artemius. months ago we had lived one monsoon night together, like husband and wife, brother and sister. i searched the main cabin, the bar, the upper deck, he was not on this ship. like a comatose ghost in a white summer dress i limped through the crowds of tube top girls, muscled boys jumping to Ricky Martin's "She Bangs." four hours stranded at sea, i considered every possible option of leaving this party without dramatics. i met an old friend, a cartoonist from the *Times* who couldn't believe he was on this voyage of the damned. staring into the East River i told him i imagine all my lovers in a line-up like usual suspects. he said he dreams of building a time-ship where he can invite all the people he ever loved, still the same age he remembered them.

The Jewish Husband

her mother always told her: marry a jewish man, little Oksanka, they make the best husbands, they bring all the money home and never beat up on their wives. her father was a baggage-handler at the airport who squandered his miniscule earnings on vodka and when that ran out he drank his wife's perfume, acetone, peroxide. so it was only natural when she grew up, she tucked away her golden crucifix, abandoned easter eggs and mistletoes and started looking for a husband at the local shuls, the jewish centers, the yiddish matchmakers. she found him one day, balding, overweight, uncircumcised, who loved bacon in the morning. she climbed mountains for his affection, immersed in mikvah, took conversion classes, entertained his infinite mishpokhe. they were planning an illustrious wedding but suddenly his uncle died, the wedding had to be postponed according to the jewish law. Oksanka's desperate cry echoed in the halls of the old temple: i don't give a shit how many more of your fucking relatives die, i am still getting married, damn it.

The Barber

i found the perfect barber in the city, quick with the scissors, kind with the blow dryer, every eight weeks he trimmed my hair for a measly sixteen dollars. i enjoyed the simplicity of his old-country shop, the lack of fancy flower arrangements, the absence of Farrah Fawcett posters. one evening washing my hair in the basin, he begged for my help in a delicate private matter – he had a son who was nineteen years old and awfully shy with the opposite sex and unlearned in the ways of love and so perhaps an experienced woman like me could teach the boy a few things. i glanced in the mirror, examined my hair, eyebrows, earrings, looking for signs that could make the little Greek barber think i was some kind of mrs. Robinson or worse, Goldie Cocks. after that night i let other men in the city cut my hair, they were all terribly gay and had no virgin sons, and insisted on being called hair consultants and charged hundreds of dollars for a simple trim and a complimentary frappuccino.

Venus

he promised to babysit her grandmother for a week. anything to get away, liquor stores and speakeasies haunted him, drinking buddies beckoned and repulsed. he fled Rhode Island, moved into her parents' house, lugging her five business suits, six dvds, a frightened cat. upon meeting her grandmother, he kissed her hand, addressing her my dearest respectable old lady. alone in the droning hours of day, he asked for her granddaughter's hand in marriage, timidly, out of boredom, then changed his mind. they slept in her parents' bedroom on the posturepedic mattress, indifferent to each other, this city, that city, ignorant of time of day, season, century, he felt her knee stabbing him in the back. she had her friends over for tea, he imagined charging each an entry fee. her parents returned with a suntan, a thermos for her, a Bermuda t-shirt for him, but he was already on the Greyhound back. it took them some time to realize that all the vodka in the fridge, the cognac in pretty gift boxes, all the wines, even the decorative naked Venus, he drank it all and refilled them with water, apple juice, some with grape juice to match the real color.

Crime and Conchitta

Lucas came by my house to borrow a copy of *Crime and Punishment* assigned to us in world literature class, suggested we watch the movie version first. leisurely we strolled to his apartment on a quiet Sunday night in Bensonhurst, an Italian neighborhood known for its safety and cleanliness. as we turned the corner a man in a baseball cap leaped out of a moving car, pointed a silver gun at us, grabbed Lucas's jacket and my backpack full of books and sped away. glued to the sidewalk aghast, speechless, we tried to make sense of the crime that took less than four seconds. Lucas was sure the man was black in a gold Chevrolet, i swore he was hispanic in a maroon Ford Taurus. when the two masculine New York's finest showed up at Lucas's house he shared with his sister, a supermodel from Naples, they didn't believe a word we said, instead they sat in the kitchen analyzing Conchitta's portfolio, critiquing runway photos and bikini shots, as we served tea and cannoli. somewhere out there was a thief with a silver gun, reading my *Crime and Punishment.*

Anchal Fabrics

i went to the silk and chiffon store on Neptune Avenue early Saturday morning. past the mosque and the Pakistani grocery, Anchal Fabrics on the corner was the size of a Queens kitchen. it was terribly crowded, women in caftans, jelabas, saris, with children in strollers and walking children, the height of a knee. all of them touching the lisping lace, caressing the atlas fabrics, measuring silk with rulers, cutting chiffon with scissors. i was looking for purple tulle to add to my discount skirt, hoping that one day there would be a cool callused hand taking it off. all of us looking for beauty, for color, vineyard green, blue bonnet, autumn gold, to become dazzling, tempting to someone's eye. giggling and blushing, they spoke the language of cotton and biryani, but for once i understood them completely. we were all women, the same, the smoking emancipators, the silent fatimas.

Corset Money

i was buying a bra at the lingerie boutique on Brighton Beach Avenue. there was no one at the register. three salesgirls were in the fitting room performing something of a Matisse's dance around a half-naked slender Russian girl. she was trying on sexy little things made of satin, silk, velvet and midnight lace imported from France and Venezuela with names like secret embrace and infinity edge. corsets, camisoles, teddies, garter belts, leopard panties, and rhinestone bras were rushed to the fitting room on overpriced hangers for eye candy's approval or immaculate veto. i wondered about this girl, she must have a very passionate and very wealthy papik since even the most unassuming thong constructed of three shoelaces and a nylon strip was priced at two hundred dollars. i waited for the pretty girl to fling her papik's unlimited American Express across the register, instead she pulled out an old fanny pack and quietly counted three thousand dollars in crumpled single dollar bills.

Pirozhok

pirozhok of '94 haunted me for years. that August, me and my friend Chip went out for a midnight swim. happy and sodden, we strolled on the boardwalk past oceanfront cafes and cabarets of festive summer people enjoying their napoleons, eclairs. Chip stopped to buy himself a pirozhok, a scrumptious russian pastry filled with cheese. i asked if he could buy me one, he said no, you can have a bite of mine. appalled, i vented to everyone i knew until the pirozhok of '94 became bigger than life, a legend repeated at parties, a chorus of guests singing you can have a bite of mine. friends had to intervene, preached it's a different century, time to let go of things collected in the nineties, Chip is a handsome successful banker now you should give him another chance. we sat on the bench in Tribeca, talking, laughing, i felt the grudge of pirozhok leaving me, slowly, quietly, no longer potent, then Chip turned and asked me for a quarter, he wanted to buy a banana from a street vendor but hated to break a dollar.

Gypsy Punk Ska

Mitch was okay. in his late thirties he looked okay, had an okay career in financial computing, okay co-op, okay jeep, okay girlfriend who was older and looked like Ingrid Bergman, but somehow he always seemed lost, like he forgot himself under the seat on the bus, disappeared in the shopping cart at the supermarket, dropped in the sand like loose change. then one day he stopped, quit and sold everything, told his woman that he loved her but he loved Gogol Bordello more, they were a gypsy-punk-ska band of fantastic hooligans from Eastern Europe. it started out slowly, he bought a ticket to their show, a CD, a DVD, then another ticket, ten more tickets until he barged in backstage, vowed his undying passion and volunteered to serve them in the name of gypsy punk ska. the musicians were dumbfounded but allowed him to run their errands, bring them vodka, line up groupies for the after-party. over time he became indispensable, they took him on tour from LA to Belfast. bunking in a sleeper bus with roadies he didn't have a penny to his name, but it did not matter because he was never okay again.

Gogi Walked Down the Street

Gogi, a puny architecture student from Tbilisi, came to America on a heavyweight wrestler's visa. he found a bed in the cellar on a dead-end street on Brighton, with eight other men sleeping in shifts. he handed out flyers advertising twenty-five cent peep shows, washed dishes at Rasputin, folded laundry at the local drop-off, he was a plumber's helper, a roof fixer, a toilet cleaner. he lived on ramen noodles, rice and beans, in desperate times he tried cat food with mustard. in the winter things got really bad, landlord changed locks without warning, plumber skipped town without paying. Gogi walked down the street, freezing, starving, an old Cadillac rolled up, give me all your money motherfucker shouted the driver, waving his gun like a ladies' handkerchief. Gogi groped in his pockets, shrugged, then hopped in the car and proposed they do this together, as partners, and if they go to jail no problem, a roof over their heads and three meals a day. the mugger scowled at the scrawny immigrant, lowered his gun, screamed, get out of the car, get out, and get a job, man, get a job.

once the head of a hospital, Sam immigrated at that age when it was too late to start over, too early to retire. a home attendant in Brooklyn, he was now assigned to D'ada Mbabaali, an exiled president of Mugembo. he helped him bathe, dress, prepared his meals, picked up prescriptions, escorted him to hearings at the United Nations, conferences, summits. D'ada introduced Samuel to foreign leaders as his trusted ally, soon he appointed him the Secretary of External Affairs and awarded him a baby elephant, awaiting in Mugembo upon the triumphant return of democracy. letters from the caretaker arrived every week with status reports, photos of the growing Kofi Samuél, showering himself with his trunk, raising his big foot in a dance. in the company of friends, other émigrés, taxi drivers, washers, handlers, Sam joked that he was now a high government official, but sometimes he secretly hoped for a coup d'état that would restore his patient to power. they would all go to Mugembo, he would ride atop his elephant while his wife, tired bitter Sarachka, would stroll the fields like Angelina Jolie, surrounded by african children and bustling bees.

eighty-eight years of steel. war, depression, another war, atomic bomb, Vietnam, raising three children, her husband's Alzheimer's. nothing could break her until her brother's death. he died with millions. mourners kissed both her cheeks, praised the dearly departed wondering how much money the old bastard left and to whom? she was convinced she would inherit it all, her brother hated everyone and had no children. four feet eight inches tall ninety two pounds, she frequented beauty parlors, shopped for fashionable undergarments in rainbow colors, spent hours on the phone with her son going over her brother's assets. not even a scream of the blackbird nor a black cat crossing the street could spoil her stainless destiny, her guaranteed happiness. she waited. her son waited. a mob of grieving relatives waited. in his will her brother bequeathed all his riches to his dead wife's niece living in Tel Aviv. the merciless corrupt patriarch didn't leave his own sister a lilliputian crumb. she was rushed to the hospital with a heart attack, her son followed after with a stroke.

Cingular

i called the cellular support desk, asked them to turn off the text-messaging feature on two of the three phones in my family plan. an agent with a southern twang said she'll be happy to assist me, adding how wonderful it is to see responsible adults exercising their parental control options, teenagers today are out of control, they don't read don't listen don't learn don't respect don't clean, all they care about is texting and sexting. i clarified that the two phones on this account belong to my parents, not my children, and they are kind of old country, still in the voicemail-training stage and use their phones mostly in supermarkets to call each other from different aisles, did you get five cloves of garlic, no? i could hear the grave disappointment on the other end, so i said you are absolutely right – teenagers today are a horror, my kid doesn't have a cell phone, not even allowed within a mile of that thing. by the time i finished my performance and hung up the phone i was so worked-up that i wanted to kill my difficult child.

Mr. Money

i decided to neuter my cat. there was no other way. living on the sixth floor of an apartment complex, i would have to hire some perky hooker-cats or join a breeding league to provide him with a normal sex life. in white slippers and a white bow tie, always dressed to the nines in his furry tuxedo, he lay curled on my lap as i dialed the neighborhood animal clinic. the mousy secretary squealed in my ear, what is the patient's name? i gave her my name. she said, you are not the patient, what's the patient's name? Mulya, i whispered. spell that, she commanded. i don't know, M-U-L-Y-A, like money in arabic. she snickered, you named your cat money, have you no shame? waiting in a reception area among posters for cat aerobics and lion haircuts, i shuddered at the familiar squeal – Mulya Rubin, who is here to pick up Mulya Rubin? as i raised my hand, flipping the middle finger, ready to scream he is not my father, nor my son, she wheeled out my Mulya Rubin, bandaged like a contused soldier.

The Man Who Lived Here Before

there were rumors that he was dying of AIDS, the days burning away like petrol, he was becoming disheveled, transparent, losing weight, walking with a cane, never saying good morning, never holding the door, but still he brought home young spanish boys, seduced them with mysterious cocktails, stories of summertime, chestnut oils, vinyl albums of Billie Holiday, Charlie Parker. at night he was seen standing in his doorway wrapped in a white silky cloak like Lucifer, bidding farewell to each unassuming lamb with a kiss on the forehead. neighbors reported there were stacks of curled *New York Times* at his doorstep before the super finally came with a crowbar, found him dead in his bed with an open Kerouac book. we came later, much later to poetic rumors and elevator whispers, but all we knew of the man who lived here before was the ceiling, painted charcoal blue with fluorescent stars, like a newborn's nursery.

The Collector

since the refinery nurse went away on maternity leave i was to take over some of her responsibilities; in addition to recruiting, i was to collect urine samples from the new hires and current employees subject to random drug testing. my first day, ankle-deep in urine, i fired a new hire Tim Zolt for smuggling into the bathroom what looked like someone else's urine in an evian spring water bottle. Jesus Lopes, an electrician from local thirty handed me a sample that was frosty cold, i remembered we had turned off the hot water to prevent creative users from diluting their urine. a disgruntled machinist James Cook, who had tested positive for cocaine twice demanded to be re-tested, claiming he was framed, he has never used cocaine, can't even spell cocaine. at the end of the day i sat in my office, team player, self-starter, polishing my summa cum laude medal, wondering if my one-hundred-thousand-dollars-in-loans education had really paid off.

Socks

i come to work with a duffle bag, sweatpants, running shoes, but the socks are missing. i ask my friends in cubicles, the Equinox, the Lucille Roberts lovers, if anyone has an extra pair. during lunch i splurge on K-mart socks, when i return a surprise pack of athletic four is sitting on my desk. i pick up food from the fridge, the strawberry crunch salad that i brought from home is bow-tied with cold Adidas socks. then a sudden intercom announcement – someone left socks in the ladies room. while i run to pick them up, another pair is laid out on my keyboard in the shape of a rose, pink nylon socks hang from the phone receiver. later an urgent delivery, box the size of HDTV, inside – one mickey mouse sock. all day long socks, socks, ankle socks, knee-hi socks, ventilator socks, some new, some worn with holes and smell of feet, spring up everywhere, in conference rooms, in office supply closets, like snow balls, like ping pong balls. a running joke for the night, i leave the office with socks to last me a lifetime but the joke is on them, my coworker-pranksters, next time i will ask for panties.

Vigilante

Ivan Razvalkin, a Russian covert operative turned American computer programmer, found a job at a small retail company in Manhattan. three days later he got fired because allegedly he applied war interrogation tactics to gather data from the users. but Ivan didn't go gently, before security escorted him out he deleted the entire database then escaped through the back door carrying the heart of the company on a floppy disk. next day the business of the firm was in a state of Hiroshima, the database that housed all the sales, shipping, distribution, and accounting was gone. the CEO received a ransom note demanding that an envelope containing fifty thousand dollars in unmarked bills be left under an oak tree sixty-five meters from exit eleven off the belt parkway at exactly 0600. when the FBI's operations unit Rescue Database captured Ivan Razvalkin at the designated pick-up position, launching floppy disks in the air he screamed, power to the programmers.

The Ear

Gertie joined our firm a year ago, an odd bird, she didn't fit into our cliquish ultra-sleek environment. in her ill-fitting garb from another era, she could have been thirty or sixty, anyone's guess. one gloomy Monday, as our glamour girls discussed their dates, double dates, pity dates, make-up sex, Gertie suddenly declared she too had a blind date once. he was nineteen, from Canada, they took the train to Central Park, he bounced off the walls and ceiling, climbed the poles like a stripper, hung off the handrails making grimaces and noises. she felt like she was on a date with a monkey. then he stuck his tongue in her ear, it felt surprisingly good. decades later, she saw Jim Carrey do it to Craig Ferguson on the show *In Living Color,* she recognized him right away, quick browse on Wikipedia confirmed that he was here that summer of '81, auditioning for *Saturday Night Live*. stunned, we stood around Gertie, like make-up artists at the Henri Bendel counter. by lunchtime the news had spread from the mail room to the executive board, everyone was talking about Jim Carrey, rushing off to see Gertie's ear, everyone called her Gertrude now.

Human Resources

on the thirty-eighth floor of the New York City conglomerate i received a tip from a confidential informant that a certain Sonia from Accounting smells like rotten eggs and poisoned herring. i summoned the Mozambique émigré to my office, she arrived with a notepad and a pencil. in my most sensitive, diplomatic manner i tried to tell her that personal hygiene is an integral part of American corporate culture, that it affects productivity and team dynamics. she looked at me, took notes, nodding, smiling, not understanding. i tried to put it in layman's terms that there seems to be some body odor problem, perhaps more showers are necessary, stronger deodorant. as the sweet Mozambique Sonia sobbed in my arms, i wanted to tell her that i was so sorry, that i detest this job more than she can imagine, that in my homeland people snitched on their neighbors and friends for their anti-Communist views, here they report on each other's bad hygiene.

Ted Timothy

Ted Timothy was looking for a new job. he was an old-timer at IBM and would have stayed there forever but his wife wanted him to make mucho dinero so our placement agency found him a gig at an internet start-up. five weeks later on Friday the start-up went under. on Monday Ted showed up in our office wearing a suit, tie, and suspenders and asked to use our copy machine. he was back on Tuesday in a different suit to fax resumes and check job listings. before we knew it he was in our office every day 9am sharp, walking the halls, laughing by the water cooler, helping secretaries with filing, eating lunch with us in the cafeteria. we grew to adore him as if he was our mascot, we wanted to keep him but the managers said there were rules, regulations, classified information. three months later he was wandering the streets of financial district in a pouring rain, slouched in his brown overcoat, still wearing the three-piece suit, working up the courage to tell Mrs. Timothy he lost his job.

The Imposter

i found Murali Kumar on Careerbuilder, intelligent, articulate, professional, a Lotus Notes ace from Cincinnati. he passed the technical phone screen with the client like a Russian ice-skater at the Olympics. accepting an offer he yessed me to death, yes i can do this job with my eyes closed, yes i can hit the ground running. on Monday morning i received a call from the client – Murali Kumar is here but i doubt he is the guy i interviewed over the phone, this one barely speaks English, no clue about Lotus Notes. gripping my heart i phoned the imposter – who are you and what are you doing at my client site? a frail pint-size voice, like dewdrops from a lotus flower flowed in streams of broken English, yes me Murali, yes lotus notes. thirty minutes of his yeses and my nos, i learned the real ace from Cincinnati was helping his New Jersey nitwit cousin get a job. sometime after lunch i heard the nitwit cousin was running down the hill from the client complex, pressing his attaché case to his chest.

Lotus Notes: software platform

Bunny Slippers

Bernard Frisk was a sweater. you could hear him sweating on the other line as he called every day to inquire, stammering and stuttering if i had found him a suitable position. i took pity on the poor chap, called in a few favors, placed him as a help desk support virtuoso with an old client at Chase Bank. a couple of months later i got a call from his manager, a compassionate humble man who i sensed was a sweater as well, in a trembling sticky voice he requested if i could possibly when i get a chance speak to Bernard about his attire, he's been coming to work in bunny slippers, blue and furry, with big protruding ears and buttons for eyes, it's been disturbing some of the bankers and senior executives Bernard supports. i dialed the looney tunes employee immediately, started screaming what kind of cotton-tails bunny hop farm are you running, this is a major bank. in the black vacuum of circuits i heard a familiar whisper, i got a terrible foot fungus, nothing fits, only bunny slippers are suitable.

The Coat

it was gone. the bald CPA was shuffling hangers back and forth in a frenzy. i tried to console him that all businessmen wore the same black wool coat, someone must have taken his by mistake. but the visitor snapped that it was a double-breasted Waffen-SS leather coat with a belt, a real classic. i nodded sympathetically, slowly taking stock of his shaved head, the square toes, yellow stitches of Doc Martens, two dozen lonely holes in his earlobes. between balance sheets and corporate tax returns i imagined him thrashing his head at a skinhead concert, fucking his girlfriend underneath a red banner with a swastika. apologizing profusely i put him in a cab, promised to find the coat, punish the criminal. then i walked the halls, looked inside the offices, glass training rooms, wondering who was responsible? the thieves, were they secret Neo-Nazis who coveted the iconic coat, or grandchildren of the Holocaust who cringed when they saw it hanging in the closet? or maybe the coat walked off by itself, took the elevator down, heil hitlered everyone in the reception, got into a sidecar of an old NSKK motorcycle and rode off, like it never happened.

Excerpts from the Office Diary

they waited until the workaholics left and the janitors collected the last of the trash. he came with a pink rose and an accordion of condoms. at first they did it on the long mahogany table in the glass conference room, her skirt hiked up, breasts bouncing inside the blouse, pearls. they tried the revolving leather chair in the controller's office with her riding on top, then bent over on a windowsill, staring out at the stains of Manhattan skyline. he kept his socks on. they worried that there might be cameras everywhere but it only added to their excitement. they finished against the employee bulletin board, push-pinned newsletters, photos from the corporate parties, people in a boat, teamwork. next morning he called, said he had a great time but also some money, forty dollars or so, must have fallen out of his pocket, if she could check the offices. so ironic, he said, like he came and paid for sex. she put him on hold, filed her nails, finished her breakfast, then picked up and with joy and exhilaration said that she found it, forty, yes, by the copy machine, here they are.

The Lamp

my co-worker Lynnette Flannigan gave me a lava lamp for my birthday. it was wrong, it could never fit into the subtle glamour of my museum-like home. i found some old bubble wrap, a blue box, tied it with a red velvet ribbon and offered it to my friend Virginia for Easter. Virginia sized up the lamp in less than ten seconds and figured that with two kids under five it had the shelf life of a dairy product so she gave it to her next-door neighbor Helena as a welcome to the co-op present. an interior decorator, Helena Green was aghast at the sheer gaudiness of the thing but knew someone who would absolutely love it, her brother-in-law Gabriel, a fingerpaint artist turned haiku poet from the Bronx. always strapped for cash, sad Gabriel regifted it to Mrs. Hashka, his Gotham writers' workshop teacher and my alumni university advisor who one day for Christmas handed me an eerily familiar blue box, tied with a tattered red velvet ribbon. as i watched the psychedelic blobs rise and fall inside the liquid, i wondered how something so wrong could suddenly seem so right.

Acknowledgments

The author wishes to thank the editors of the following publications, where some of these pieces previously have appeared in slightly different form:

Mudfish, Skidrow Penthouse, Poetica, Knee Jerk, Jersey Devil, Ginosko, California Quarterly, Sacramento Poetry, Imitation Fruit, Cavalier, Gander Press, Dos Pasos, Clark Street Review, Willard & Maple, NAP, Zygote in My Coffee, Pinch Journal, Abbey, The 13th Warrior, Jewish Women's Literary Journal, White Pelican Review, Aphros, Madhatters Review, Portland Review, Lady Churchill's Wristlet, Muse Café, Hobo Pancakes, Coal City Review, Underground Voices, Wild Violet, The Green Hills Lantern, Nerve Cowboy, Blue Collar Review, Asinine Review, The Boiler Journal, 13 Miles from Cleveland, Subterranean Journal, Nano Fiction, Yes Poetry, The Boiler Journal, and *Thumbnail Magazine.*

With gratitude, the author offers thanks to the following individuals who played an important role in this book's creation:

Jill Hoffman and the Mudfish workshop, Stephanie Dickinson, Michael Montlack, Jane Klikfeld who read these pieces when they were rambling skeletons and saw them for what they could be, Audrey Chernoff for her impeccable taste, Edymari De Leon for being my crash test dummy read, the 2013 Blueprint Fellowship cohort, Lois and Ricky, the gang at Starpoint, Jennifer Joseph – my publisher who vetoed every bad idea i had to turn this into a delectable collection, Philip Volkers for his delicious cover, my amazing parents and friends who inspire me to write and to live every day. Thank you.

The author gratefully acknowledges that this project was made possible through a generous grant by the BluePrint Fellowship project of COJECO, funded by the UJA-Federation of New York and Genesis Philanthropy Group.

About the Author

Marina Rubin was born in the small town of Vinnitsa, Ukraine, in the former Soviet Union. Her family immigrated to United States in 1989 seeking political asylum. After months of living in refugee camps in Austria and Italy, the family arrived in New York. Marina attended New Utrecht High School where she discovered her passion for writing and became a poetry editor of the school literary magazine. Upon graduating, she earned that year's only award for Excellence in Creative Writing. With a writing scholarship from the United Federation of Teachers, she attended Pace University in New York City and graduated with a degree in Psychology. While a student she won numerous university awards for poetry. Traveling through Europe, Scandinavia, Africa and Middle East became an infinite source of inspiration for the young author. Her first chapbook *Ode to Hotels* (2002) was followed by *Once* (2004) and *Logic* (2007). Rubin is an associate editor of *Mudfish,* the Tribeca literary and art magazine. Her work was nominated for the Pushcart Prize in 2007 and 2012. She is a 2013 recipient of the COJECO Blueprint Fellowship.